SKYLARK CHOOSE YOUR OWN ADVENTURE® · 18

"I DON'T LIKE CHOOSE YOUR OWN ADVENTURE® BOOKS. I *LOVE* THEM!" says Jessica Gordon, age 10. And now, kids between the ages of 6 and 9 can choose their own adventure, too. Here's what kids have to say about the Skylark Choose Your Own Adventure® books.

"These are my favorite books because you can pick whatever choice you want—and the story is all about you."

—**Katy Alson,** *age 8*

"I love finding out how my story will end."

—**Joss Williams,** *age 9*

"I like all the illustrations!"

—**Savitri Brightfield,** *age 7*

"A six-year-old friend and I have lots of fun making the decisions together."

—**Peggy Marcus** *(adult)*

Bantam Skylark Books in the Choose Your Own
   Adventure® Series
Ask your bookseller for the books you have missed

#1 THE CIRCUS

#2 THE HAUNTED HOUSE

#3 SUNKEN TREASURE

#4 YOUR VERY OWN ROBOT

#5 GORGA, THE SPACE MONSTER

#6 THE GREEN SLIME

#7 HELP! YOU'RE SHRINKING

#8 INDIAN TRAIL

#9 DREAM TRIPS

#10 THE GENIE IN THE BOTTLE

#11 THE BIGFOOT MYSTERY

#12 THE CREATURE FROM MILLER'S POND

#13 JUNGLE SAFARI

#14 THE SEARCH FOR CHAMP

#15 THE THREE WISHES

#16 DRAGONS!

#17 WILD HORSE COUNTRY

#18 SUMMER CAMP

SUMMER CAMP

JUDY GITENSTEIN

ILLUSTRATED BY TED ENIK

An Edward Packard Book

A BANTAM SKYLARK BOOK®

TORONTO · NEW YORK · LONDON · SYDNEY · AUCKLAND

RL 2, 007–009

SUMMER CAMP

A Bantam Skylark Book / July 1984
Skylark Books is a registered trademark of Bantam Books, Inc.

CHOOSE YOUR OWN ADVENTURE® is a registered
trademark of Bantam Books, Inc. Registered in U.S. Patent
and Trademark Office and elsewhere.

Front cover art by Paul Granger

Original conception of Edward Packard

ISBN 0-553-15262-9

Published simultaneously in the United States and Canada

Bantam Books are published by Bantam Books, Inc. Its trade-
mark, consisting of the words "Bantam Books" and the por-
trayal of a rooster, is Registered in U.S. Patent and Trademark
Office and in other countries. Marca Registrada. Bantam
Books, Inc., 666 Fifth Avenue, New York, New York 10103.

PRINTED IN THE UNITED STATES OF AMERICA

CW   0 9 8 7 6 5 4 3 2 1

*To all my friends
at Bantam*

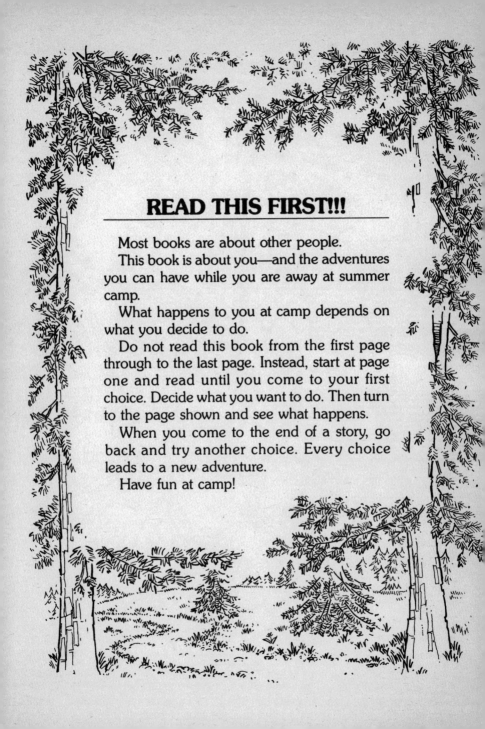

READ THIS FIRST!!!

Most books are about other people.

This book is about you—and the adventures you can have while you are away at summer camp.

What happens to you at camp depends on what you decide to do.

Do not read this book from the first page through to the last page. Instead, start at page one and read until you come to your first choice. Decide what you want to do. Then turn to the page shown and see what happens.

When you come to the end of a story, go back and try another choice. Every choice leads to a new adventure.

Have fun at camp!

The day you've been waiting for all year is **1** finally here. It's your first day of summer camp. You've never been away from home before. Now you'll be gone for two months!

You've just said goodbye to your family at the station, and you and lots of other kids are riding on the camp bus.

Sitting next to you is a girl named Terry. "This is my second summer at camp," she tells you. "When we get there, I can show you all around."

The bus ride takes most of the day. Finally you reach the dirt road that leads to camp. Soon you pass through the main gate.

You and Terry and the rest of the kids crowd to the front of the bus. "We're here!" everyone shouts.

Turn to page 2.

2   The bus stops in front of the Main Lodge, and everyone jumps off.

Lots of campers have already arrived. Some are saying hello to their friends from last year. Some are just standing around, looking lost. You're glad you're with Terry.

A group of kids is standing around a man near the flagpole. "There's Ed," says Terry. "He's our head counselor. He'll tell us what cabins we're in."

You and Terry wait in line until it's your turn. "Welcome to camp!" Ed says to you. He flips through the list on his clipboard. "You and Terry are both in Cabin Six."

"Great!" says Terry. "Now I can show you around. But we don't have to do that right away. We can go to our cabin first. Maybe some other kids will be there. Which do you want to do?"

If you decide to go right to your cabin, turn to page 4.

If you decide you want to see what camp looks like, turn to page 6.

4   "I'd like to go to our cabin," you say to Terry.

Cabin Six is a big log house with a boys' side and a girls' side. Lots of kids are on the porch when you arrive. Terry introduces you to B.J. and Laura, two girls from last summer. Terry also knows your counselor, Joan. "We're lucky," Terry whispers to you. "She'll let us do *anything.*"

Inside, you find your trunk and stack your clothes on the wooden shelves. "We have to be really neat," Terry tells you. "If you don't make your bed, our cabin will lose points in inspection."

"Ugh," you think. But you smooth the corners and roll your extra blanket neatly at the end of your bed.

Just as you finish, you hear a bugle in the distance. "That's first call for dinner," Joan says.

You and your new cabinmates run up the hill to the dining hall.

Turn to page 18.

6   "I'd like to see what camp looks like," you say.

"Okay," says Terry. "Get ready for the special tour. Follow me!"

Terry does somersaults all the way down the hill. "You'll be able to do that by the end of the summer!" she calls. You hope so.

Terry shows you all around camp. Finally you come to the edge of the woods. "Let's not go any farther," Terry says.

"Why not?" you ask.

"There's poison ivy in there. Plus," Terry **7** whispers, "last year everyone talked about the man who lives all alone in a cave in the woods. He's supposed to be a hermit. I never saw him myself, but a few of the boys said they saw him walking around one night."

A rabbit darts across the path that leads into the woods. Suddenly you feel very cold.

"Let's get out of here," you say.

Turn to page 10.

You decide to play shortstop.   **9**

By the last inning, your team is ahead by one point. "We can't let them get any more runs," Buzz says to you.

The next batter hits a fly ball. The whole team watches as the ball soars high up in the air. Then it starts to land. It's coming right at you!

"Get it!" yells Buzz. You look up, but all you can see is yellow spots. The sun is shining right in your eyes. You run back and forth underneath the spot where you think the ball is going to come down.

Smack! The ball lands in your glove. You've caught it!

"OUT!"

"Nice work, Shorty," says Buzz. "Maybe we'll sign you up for our team."

Terry runs over to you after the game. "That was a great catch!" she says. "I'm glad we're in the same cabin."

Turn to page 28.

You and Terry race back down the road. When you reach the Main Lodge, you see Ed with another group of campers. You feel much better.

You and Terry pass the infirmary and the shower house. "You'll get used to the freezing-cold showers soon!" she says with a laugh.

Just beyond the soccer field, you see a group of kids playing softball. You can also see some kids at the archery range.

"Sports!" shouts Terry. "Which one do you want to try?"

You love to play softball, but archery looks like fun, too.

If you decide to play softball, turn to page 20.

If you decide to try archery, turn to page 16.

12   You decide to sign up for the horseback ride.

You go to riding class every morning. After a few weeks, you've learned to walk and trot in the ring.

One day you arrive at the stable to find the horses lined up outside the ring. Suzy, your instructor, tells the group that you're ready for the big trip. "We're going to follow the trail all the way out to the waterfall. Then we'll have our picnic lunch and a swim," she says.

Suzy gives everyone a choice of horses. You get to choose between Butterscotch and Cannonball.

You're not sure which horse to pick. You've ridden Butterscotch a few times. She's a good horse, but she's also fat and slow. Cannonball is a beautiful horse, but he's very fast. Cannonball might be dangerous!

If you pick Butterscotch, turn to page 31.

If you pick Cannonball, turn to page 37.

"I'd like to be catcher," you say.

Terry stays out in the field. You walk over to home plate. You put on the catcher's mask and kneel down, ready for the first pitch.

"Let's warm up," Buzz calls.

Buzz throws a fast ball that stings your hand through your glove. The next pitch is so fast that you barely see the ball coming. It zooms by you and lands in the bushes behind home plate.

It takes you a long time to find the ball. "What a baby!" yells Buzz. "I thought you said you could play."

When the game finally starts, you have a new position—water boy!

The End

"I'd like to try archery," you tell Terry.

"Great!" she says. "Archery is my favorite sport. I'll show you how to shoot."

Terry grips the bow tightly in one hand and rests the arrow gently across it. She raises the bow and pulls the string back to just below her chin. Then she closes one eye and stands very

still for a moment. When she lets go of the arrow, it soars through the air and lands in the center of the target.

Bull's-eye!

"Now you try it," Terry says as she hands you the bow and arrow.

Turn to page 52.

18   The dining hall is crowded and noisy when you arrive. Joan serves everyone at your table spaghetti and meatballs, salad, rolls, and milk.

Go on to the next page.

The food tastes terrible!

Laura twirls some spaghetti around her fork. "They don't make me eat worms at home," she says.

B.J. starts to giggle. "Let's see if this meatball will bounce," she says.

"Don't you dare!" yells Joan. But she's laughing, too, so you know she isn't angry.

You're eating your ice cream when Ed stands up to make the announcements. "Tonight is an important night," he says. "Tonight we sign up for the special trips we'll be taking during the summer."

You listen eagerly as Ed describes the choices. There's an overnight mountain-climbing trip, an all-day canoe trip, and a horseback ride and picnic.

They all sound like fun!

If you decide to go on the mountain-climbing trip, turn to page 22.

If you decide to take the canoe trip, turn to page 27.

If you decide to pick the horseback ride, turn to page 12.

19

20   "Let's play softball," you say. You and Terry run over to the game.

The pitcher is a big boy named Buzz. "We need a shortstop and a catcher," he says. "You can play if you want to. But you'd better be good. This is an important game."

*If you decide to play shortstop,
turn to page 9.*

*If you decide to be catcher,
turn to page 15.*

22   You sign up for the overnight mountain climb.

On the day of the trip, you pack your knapsack with your flashlight, a poncho, a sweater, and an extra pair of socks. Then you add some books, your diary, and your teddy bear.

When you arrive at the state park, Joan says, "Stay together! If anyone gets lost, wait where you are. We'll come get you."

You spend the whole day climbing up the trail. By afternoon, your knapsack feels so heavy that you start to walk very slowly. Soon you're at the back of the group. You bend down for a second to tie your shoelace. When you get up, the group is gone!

Joan said to stay where you are if you got lost. But it's getting late. Will the group be able to find you in the dark? Maybe you should try to catch up to them.

If you decide to wait, turn to page 43.

If you try to find the group, turn to page 49.

"Okay," you say. "We'll take you up on your dare. We'll go find the hermit."

You and Terry start off toward the hermit's cave. Your flashlight beams bounce up and down on the road as you walk. The trees look like skeletons dancing in the moonlight.

When you reach the end of the road, Terry points to a dark part of the woods. "I think his cave is in there," she says.

A shadowy figure appears right where Terry is pointing. "Who's there?" a deep voice calls.

No one answers—because you and Terry are racing back down the road.

You dive into some bushes. "This is silly," Terry says. "We shouldn't be afraid of some old hermit. Do you want to try again?"

If you say yes, turn to page 50.

If you say no, turn to page 44.

On the day of the canoe trip, the bugle **27**
wakes you early. You put on a bathing suit under your jeans and sweatshirt and meet your
group at the Main Lodge.

Everyone gets into the front of the camp
bus. The canoes are piled carefully in the back.

You sit next to a boy named Bobby. The bus
ride seems to take *forever,* so you both eat your
lunches. Then you ask what time it is. Oh, no!
Lunchtime is still hours away!

When you reach the river, you and Bobby
help Bobby's counselor, Mike, put your canoe
into the water. Mike hands you a paddle and
holds the canoe while you step into the bow.
Bobby kneels against the seat in the middle.
Then Mike gets into the stern and pushes off.

You and Mike are strong paddlers. Soon
your canoe is gliding swiftly ahead of the oth-
ers.

Turn to page 32.

28   During the summer, you and Terry become best friends. Every night, after the bugle plays taps, you stay up late telling each other jokes and scary stories.

One night you're walking back from the evening movie, *The Creature That Came From the Woods*. David and Steve, two of the boys from Cabin Six, run to catch up with you.

"Do you want to go look for the hermit?" David asks.

"No," you say.

"Why not? Are you chicken?"

"No," Terry says.

"Well, we dare you! We dare you to find the hermit!" Steve says.

You and Terry look at each other. "Do you want to?" Terry whispers.

If you say yes, turn to page 24.

If you say no, turn to page 38.

You walk over to Butterscotch and pat her **31** neck. She nuzzles you in a friendly way. "I'd like to ride her," you say.

Suzy swings up on a horse named Midnight. You tap Butterscotch lightly with your heels and take your place in line.

The horses walk single file on the road. When you reach the trail, the horses up ahead start to trot. At first you bounce in the saddle, but soon you are posting smoothly up and down.

You ride for most of the morning. At last the trail leads to a stream. You follow the stream for a few miles. Butterscotch steps carefully over the slippery rocks.

Soon you hear a roar high above you. It's the waterfall!

Turn to page 46.

After about an hour, Mike rests his paddle across the canoe. You put your hand over the side and feel the cool water as you drift downstream.

Birch trees sway in the breeze along the banks of the river. You catch sight of some deer, but they're so shy that they run away when you pass.

Just then B.J.'s canoe glides by—and then it disappears!

"We've reached the rapids!" calls Mike. "Start paddling. And watch out for the rocks."

The current is so strong that you can barely

hold your paddle. Water splashes over the bow **33** and soaks you.

"There's a rock right in front of us!" shouts Bobby.

You are terrified. That rock is huge—and it's getting closer. You wonder if you should jump out of the canoe.

If you decide to jump out, turn to page 40.

If you decide to stay in the canoe, turn to page 35.

You decide you'd better stay in the canoe. **35**

Mike fights the current with powerful strokes. Finally he's able to steer the canoe away from the rock.

But now you are headed downstream, toward the place where B.J.'s canoe disappeared. "Hang on!" Mike yells.

You and Bobby grip the sides of the canoe and close your eyes as you go down the rapids. It's like a roller coaster ride on water!

Suddenly the river is calm again. You've made it! You have passed the rapids. You paddle over to B.J.'s canoe.

Everyone cheers—except for Bobby. He is still hanging on to the side of the canoe. He looks sick.

"Next time *you're* going to paddle," Mike tells him.

"Next time *I'm* signing up for mountain climbing!" Bobby answers.

"Maybe a swim will make you feel better," you say.

And you and Mike push Bobby into the water!

The End

Cannonball stands quietly while Suzy helps you into the saddle. As you shorten your stirrups, Gumdrop, the stable cat, runs out of the ring and darts through the horse's legs. Cannonball rears and takes off down the road.

"Whoa!" you yell. You try pulling the reins hard, but that only makes Cannonball go faster. He jumps over a log that has fallen across the trail. You lean forward and hang on to his mane. Finally Cannonball stops—but you keep going.

You land in the tall grass beside the trail. Cannonball trots off as if nothing has happened.

In a minute, Suzy gallops up. "You'll be okay," she says. "Just a few scratches. You'll be back on Cannonball in no time."

That's what she thinks!

"No, thanks," you say. "I'm going to *walk* to the waterfall."

The End

38   "I don't care what they say. I don't want to find the hermit," you tell Terry.

"Good," Terry says. "I was afraid you were going to say yes."

You turn and head back to the cabin. "Watch out!" David yells. "The hermit walks around at night."

You and Terry get back to your cabin just before lights-out. You lie in the dark and try to fall asleep. The wind starts to blow outside the window, and just then you hear a scratching noise on the screen.

"Maybe that's the hermit!" you whisper.

"I hope it was just a branch," says Terry.

You will never know if there's really a hermit at camp. Maybe next year you'll try to find out.

The End

40   You jump out into the foamy water.
And that's the last thing you remember.

When you wake up, you're lying on the shore beside the river. Mike and Bobby are standing over you. You try to sit up, but your leg hurts too much.

Mike has made a splint out of your paddle. "It may be just a sprain. I'm glad you're safe," he says. "Don't you *ever* do that again."

"Don't worry!" you say.

The End

You decide to wait for the group to find you.

You lean against a tree and take a book out of your knapsack. You can hear birds chirping in the trees. A chipmunk runs across the trail.

Soon you hear a voice calling your name. Joan comes running down the trail. "Am I glad you stayed where you were. We would never have found you!" she says.

Joan takes you back to the campsite. Your tents are set up next to some tall pine trees. Some of the other campers are cooking stew over an open campfire.

You eat your dinner under the stars. Afterward, you sit around telling ghost stories. Just as you are eating your s'mores, it starts to rain.

You fall asleep, snug and dry, in your tent.

The End

44   "Let's get out of here!" you say.

You and Terry run back to the bunk. "That was a close call," she says as you climb into your beds.

The next morning, you sleep through reveille. At first call, you and Terry are still in bed. "Rise and shine!" Joan calls. She walks around to your beds and pulls down the covers. "Oh, my goodness," she says. "Where have you two been? You have the worst case of poison ivy I've ever seen."

Oh, no!

You didn't find the hermit last night. You found the poison ivy patch!

The End

46   The waterfall is beautiful.

You stop the horses and watch as the water rushes over a cliff into a pool below it.

It's much too steep and slippery to ride the rest of the way, so you tie the horses to some pine trees by the stream.

When you reach the top, you take off your riding boots and let your feet dangle in the cool water.

The horses drink from the stream in the

shade down below as you and the other riders **47**
spread out your picnic lunch on a rock in the
sun. Suzy gives you each two sandwiches, an
orange, a candy bar, and a soda.

After lunch, you swim through the pool to
the waterfall. You stand on a rock and let the
water splash over your head. This has been
your best day all summer.

The End

You decide to try and find the group.

You walk down the trail you think they took. You walk for a long time, but you don't see anyone. You're tired and thirsty. The pine needles scratch at your ankles. And the mosquitos won't stop biting you.

You start to pass familiar places along the trail. You must be walking around in circles. Now you're really lost!

Soon it starts to rain. As you huddle in your poncho under a tree, you wonder if they'll ever find you.

The End

50   "We've gone this far," you tell Terry. "We can't stop now."

You creep back down the road again.

"*Who's there?*" the voice calls again.

You shine your flashlight straight ahead. "It's David and Steve!" whispers Terry.

Quickly you turn off your flashlight. In the moonlight you can see that Steve is wearing a sheet and standing on David's shoulders.

"They're trying to scare us. They're playing a joke on us!" Terry says.

"Let's play a joke on *them*," you say.

You creep forward a little more. Suddenly you and Terry jump up and yell, "BOO!"

The boys are so surprised that they fall over.

You and Terry can't stop laughing. "Okay, we did it," you tell them. "Now we dare *you* to find the hermit!"

The End

Archery is harder than it looks! First you let go of the string too soon, and the arrow falls down at your feet.

Then you pull the string so far back that *you* fall down.

After about an hour, you're able to shoot,

but the target is so far away that your arrows don't even come close.

Finally, everyone at the archery range moves one target closer—just for you.

While everyone watches, you lift your bow, pull the string, and let go. Your arrow splits one of Terry's arrows right down the middle. It's a super-bull's-eye!

Everyone cheers. "Let's see you do that again," Terry says.

You wonder if you ever could.

The End

ABOUT THE AUTHOR

Judy Gitenstein spent seven summers at a camp in Maine very much like the one described in this book. She was for several years the editor of the Bantam Choose Your Own Adventure series and is currently the editorial director of the young readers division at Avon Books.

ABOUT THE ILLUSTRATOR

Ted Enik is a playwright and cartoonist as well as a children's book illustrator. For Bantam Books he has illustrated *Bob Fulton's Terrific Time Machine* by Jerome Beatty, Jr., the Sherluck Bones Mystery-Detective books by Jim and Mary Razzi, the Slimy's Book of Fun and Games series, *The Creature from Miller's Pond* by Susan Saunders (a Skylark Choose Your Own Adventure), and *The Curse of Batterslea Hall* by Richard Brightfield (a Choose Your Own Adventure book). Mr. Enik lives in New York City.

Now you can have your favorite Choose Your Own Adventure® Series in a variety of sizes. Along with the popular pocket size, Bantam has introduced the Choose Your Own Adventure® series in a Skylark edition and also in Hardcover.

Now not only do you get to decide on how you want your adventures to end, you also get to decide on what size you'd like to collect them in.

SKYLARK EDITIONS

☐	15238	The Circus #1 E. Packard	$1.95
☐	15207	The Haunted House #2 R. A. Montgomery	$1.95
☐	15208	Sunken Treasure #3 E. Packard	$1.95
☐	15233	Your Very Own Robot #4 R. A. Montgomery	$1.95
☐	15308	Gorga, The Space Monster #5 E. Packard	$1.95
☐	15309	The Green Slime #6 S. Saunders	$1.95
☐	15195	Help! You're Shrinking #5 E. Packard	$1.95
☐	15201	Indian Trail #8 R. A. Montgomery	$1.95
☐	15191	The Genie In the Bottle #10 J. Razzi	$1.95
☐	15222	The Big Foot Mystery #11 L. Sonberg	$1.95
☐	15223	The Creature From Millers Pond #12 S. Saunders	$1.95
☐	15226	Jungle Safari #13 E. Packard	$1.95
☐	15227	The Search For Champ #14 S. Gilligan	$1.95

HARDCOVER EDITIONS

☐	05018	Sunken Treasure E. Packard	$6.95
☐	05019	Your Very Own Robot R. A. Montgomery	$6.95
☐	05031	Gorga, The Space Monster #5 E. Packard	$7.95
☐	05032	Green Slime #6 S. Saunders	$7.95

Prices and availability subject to change without notice.

Buy them at your local bookstore or use this handy coupon for ordering:

Bantam Books, Inc., Dept. AVSK, 414 East Golf Road, Des Plaines, Ill. 60016

Please send me the books I have checked above. I am enclosing $_____ (please add $1.25 to cover postage and handling). Send check or money order—no cash or C.O.D.'s please.

Mr/Ms _____

Address _____

City/State _____ Zip _____

AVSK—6/84

Please allow four to six weeks for delivery. This offer expires 12/84.
